SPACE DETECTIVES

COSMIC PET PUZZLE

SPACE DETECTIVES

COSMIC PET PUZZLE

MARK POWERS

Illustrated by
DAPO ADEOLA

BLOOMSBURY
CHILDREN'S BOOKS
LONDON OXFORD NEW YORK NEW DELHI SYDNEY

BLOOMSBURY CHILDREN'S BOOKS
Bloomsbury Publishing Plc
50 Bedford Square, London WC1B 3DP, UK
29 Earlsfort Terrace, Dublin 2, Ireland

BLOOMSBURY, BLOOMSBURY CHILDREN'S BOOKS and the Diana logo
are trademarks of Bloomsbury Publishing Plc

First published in Great Britain in 2022 by Bloomsbury Publishing Plc

A catalogue record for this book is available from the British Library

ISBN: PB: 978-1-5266-0321-0; eBook: 978-1-5266-0323-4

2 4 6 8 10 9 7 5 3

Printed and bound in Great Britain by CPI Group (UK) Ltd, Croydon CR0 4YY

To find out more about our authors and books visit www.bloomsbury.com
and sign up for our newsletters

To Gareth Kavanagh,
happy times and places

With thanks to Jo, Kate, Zöe,
Dapo, Fran & David Slack
and all at Bloomsbury
– Mark

To all our readers, adventurers and
aspiring *Space Detectives* out there,
thank you so much for reading our books
and showing love ☺
– Dapo

PROLOGUE

What a confusing place this Starville is! thought the stranger. So different to the far-off planet it called home. While on that planet the rain fell whenever it felt like it, on the space station Starville it only ever rained on Thursday afternoons between 3.00 p.m. and 3.15 p.m. And while the stranger's planet was populated with plants it recognised, like five-leafed fire-nettles, Starville was overflowing with thousands of different species from every corner of the galaxy.

It was an awful lot to get used to.

The stranger suddenly felt very lonely. It wondered whether it would ever make any friends in this bizarre new place. *Oh well*, it thought, *I'll never know unless I try …*

Chapter 1
Smurble

'Wowowowowow!' barked Smurble, and pelted after the stick that Alfie had thrown along the leaf-strewn path.

It was a pleasant afternoon for a stroll in Starville Botanical Gardens. The sun was shining and the air was filled with the scents of flowers and plants collected from a hundred different alien worlds: little Neptunian shark-daisies, glittering rock orchids from Venus, vast elephant-sized murk-blooms from Cygnus B.

Skidding to a halt, Smurble picked up the

stick in his bill and trotted back towards his master, his long scaly tail swishing back and forth with happiness.

'Good boy!' said Alfie, wrenching the stick from Smurble's bill and ruffling the fur behind his large pointed ears. Smurble chirruped and clicked contentedly. Alfie flung the stick away again and watched as Smurble bounded happily after it, his tail sending up little blizzards of leaves.

Alfie was the first kid in his school to own a Synthpet, a fact that made him extremely proud and all his classmates extremely jealous. Synthpets were the latest craze on Starville. They were extraordinary artificial creatures made in laboratories by combining the DNA of different animals. You simply selected the animal parts you required from a long list a bit like a menu (otter's body with a rhino's head and writhing green tentacles? No problem!) and the scientists at FluffyCorp Inc pressed a few buttons on their incredible DNA-printer machine. A few seconds later, out popped whatever bizarre form of life you had requested, all ready to take home and name.

RABBIT EARS:
NOW 65%
MORE SNUGGLY!

CAT BODY:
COMES WITH
SELF-CLEANING FUR.
POOPS IN HYPERSPACE
SO NO MESS!

CROCODILE TAIL:
SIMPLY BECAUSE IT LOOKS SICK.
WHY WOULDN'T YOU?

Smurble was Alfie's Synthpet. He had the body and legs of a cat, a duck's bill, long rabbit-like ears, a pair of constantly twitching antennae and the scaly tail of a crocodile. He followed Alfie everywhere, made the strangest collection of noises Alfie had ever heard – from quacks to barks and grasshopper-like chirrups – and could do all manner of fun tricks like somersaults and walking on his hind legs. Alfie adored him.

Smurble had been a birthday present. Usually Alfie's birthday presents were nothing to get excited about – a deck of 3-D playing cards or a ticket to Starville Space Zoo. But this year, for his eleventh birthday, his parents had decided to get him something really special.

After racing back to Alfie with the stick, Smurble suddenly halted and raised his head, chirruping softly. His long antennae began to wave excitedly back and forth.

'What's up, boy?' asked Alfie. 'Can you hear something?'

He took a step towards Smurble. There was a strange rustling nearby. A large shadow loomed overhead. Alfie looked up, his eyes widening in fear and astonishment, and gave a scream as everything suddenly turned black …

Chapter 2
Smurble come home

In the *Space Detectives*' office, halfway up a gleaming skyscraper in the centre of Starville's busiest district, ten-year-old Connor Crake was staring out of the window and nervously chewing the blunt end of an electro-pencil.

He was a tallish, skinny boy with big glasses and looked a bit like an elongated owl. His nimble brain was busy trying to solve a mystery. Unusually it was a mystery of his own and not one a client had brought in.

Connor had lost his badge. It was a small, round metal badge, about the size of a medal, and had the words *World's Greatest Detective* written on it. The badge had been a gift from a girl called Nancy at Connor's primary school several years ago as a reward for finding her lost kitten.

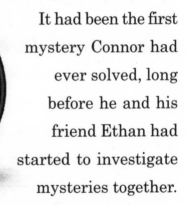

It had been the first mystery Connor had ever solved, long before he and his friend Ethan had started to investigate mysteries together.

He had treasured the badge ever since.

Adjusting his glasses with a bony finger, he racked his brain and tried to *think think think* what had happened to his badge. He'd definitely had it on last Wednesday when he and Ethan had taken a rocket bus day trip to Mars because it had made the metal detector at the spaceport bleep ...

'Found it!' cried a voice, interrupting Connor's thoughts. 'Finally! I've found it!'

Connor's friend Ethan, the other young **Space Detective**, burst into the office from the adjoining kitchen area. He was a squat, sturdily built boy with the restless energy of a scalded ferret.

'My badge?' asked Connor hopefully. 'Where was it?'

'No, not that,' said Ethan. 'I mean I've found the perfect after-lunch snack. Want to know what it is?'

'Oh,' said Connor, his smile fading. 'Not really.'

'I'll tell you anyway,' said Ethan, 'because it's pretty interesting. It's called a bacon and trifle wrap. Now, I know that *sounds* disgusting, but it's surprisingly—'

DING! DONG!

The office doorbell cut Ethan short. Connor was glad. He opened the door to find a glum-faced boy standing outside, hands thrust deep in his pockets.

'This the *Space Detectives*?'

Connor nodded. 'It is.'

'My name's Alfie Flumpleton and I need your help. Desperately.'

'So, let's get this straight,' said Connor, speedily jotting notes on his electronic pad. 'You were walking in the botanical gardens with your pet … ?'

'*Synth*pet,' Alfie corrected him. 'He's called Smurble. I'll send you his picture.'

There was a **PING!** and a photograph appeared on the screen of Connor's electronic pad. It showed Alfie smiling proudly beside an extraordinary creature seemingly made of an odd jumble of parts from different animals. Connor showed the picture to Ethan.

Ethan blinked.

17

The creature looked like something from a particularly disturbing cheese dream. It was all he could do not to make an **EURGH** face. 'And then what happened … ?'

'And then,' said Alfie, 'someone hit me on the back of the head. I didn't see who. It was all over so fast. The next thing I knew, I was waking up in a bush with an awful headache. And Smurble had gone.'

'And you're positive he hasn't just scarpered off somewhere?' asked Ethan. 'He's not hiding anywhere in the botanical gardens, for example?'

Alfie rolled his eyes. 'I looked absolutely *everywhere!*' he groaned. 'There was no sign of him at all.'

Connor adjusted his glasses thoughtfully. 'Aren't all pets on Starville meant to be microchipped? You know, those little electronic chips implanted in them so they can be found or identified if they get lost?'

Alfie nodded. 'Yes, Smurble has been microchipped. And I'm supposed to be able to track him with this.' He showed Connor a snazzy-looking watch with a large screen strapped to his wrist. On it was a map of Starville steeped in a bright green glow.

'And what does it say?' asked Connor.

'It says the signal from the microchip has been muffled somehow. According to the watch, Smurble's definitely *somewhere* on Starville, but it can't be any more precise than that.'

'Ah well,' said Ethan. 'At least that narrows it down a bit.'

'Yeah, to a few hundred square kilometres,' muttered Alfie with a sigh. 'You've got to help me, guys. Someone's kidnapped Smurble, I just know it. And I miss the little dude *so* much.'

'Who knows you own Smurble?' asked Connor.

Alfie gave a snort. 'Just about everyone I know. As soon as my mum and dad gave him to me, I sent that picture of me and Smurble to all my family and every kid in school.'

Ethan grinned. 'Couldn't resist bragging, eh?'

'Too right!' said Alfie. 'Having a Synthpet is a *huge* deal. They're so cool right now and there's a massive waiting list to get one. You'd have done the same.'

Ethan nodded. 'Maybe. But your showing

off might have given lots of people a motive to take Smurble.'

Alfie frowned as Connor scratched the tip of his chin thoughtfully. 'I take it Smurble is the only one of his kind – I mean the only Synthpet with this combination of animal parts?'

Alfie nodded. 'Yes, he's absolutely unique. The company guaranteed it.'

Connor made a note. 'Hmm. Interesting. That means whoever stole Smurble can't parade him about in public like a normal pet because he'd be recognised.'

Ethan raised his eyebrows at Connor. 'So what do you reckon?'

Connor got to his feet. 'I reckon we need to visit the scene of the crime.'

Chapter 3
Scene of the crime

The botanical gardens were quiet when the three boys arrived. They paid their entrance fees to a small blue anteater in the ticket booth who was feeding its pet turtle under the counter. Ethan showed the anteater a photo of Smurble on his electronic notepad.

'Do you remember seeing a creature like this in here yesterday?'

The anteater grunted in irritation and squinted at the image on Ethan's pad. It shook its long, pointed nose. 'You know how many visitors this place gets each day? Hundreds and hundreds. You can't expect me to remember one single –' he frowned at the image of Smurble – 'whatever *that* is.'

'It's a Synthpet,' said Connor. 'A very valuable one. And it's missing. So do you mind if we check your security camera feed from yesterday?'

The anteater gave a shrug. 'If you must.' It tapped a key on the computer in its booth. 'There. I've sent all yesterday's CCTV footage to your device.'

'Thanks!'

Alfie and Ethan huddled around Connor's electronic notepad. The screen showed four different locations in the gardens.

'Scroll forward to about half past two in the afternoon,' said Ethan, checking his notes. 'That's when it happened.'

Connor ran his finger along the screen and the video raced forward in time.

'There!' said Alfie. 'Stop! That's me and Smurble.'

Connor took his finger off the screen. The three of them watched as images of Alfie and Smurble appeared in one location, Smurble yapping and scampering around Alfie's ankles as the boy picked up a stick and threw it along the path.

'It must be about now!' said Alfie, his eyes wide with excitement. 'I remember throwing that stick for him ...'

But at that moment a large green blur appeared on the video image, blotting out Alfie and Smurble.

'I don't get it,' said Alfie. 'What's happening?'

'I expect a leaf must have blown over the camera lens,' said Connor. 'That's a bit of bad luck. I'll fast-forward.'

He scrolled through the video image. Eventually the green blur disappeared, but all that was left on the video was the image of Alfie lying unconscious on the ground amid the vegetation.

Ethan groaned. 'We've missed the crucial moment!'

Connor pocketed his notepad. He looked at Alfie thoughtfully. 'Take us to where it happened.'

Alfie led them along one of the wide stone paths that snaked between the displays of Martian stinging parsnips, murk-blooms from Cygnus B and other weird vegetation. The only sound apart from their footsteps was the faint hum of insect wings high above in the leafy canopy formed by the criss-crossing branches of huge alien trees.

'You don't think it's possible that Smurble just pushed you into a bush and ran away?' asked Ethan. 'He's a strange new creature. Who knows what he was thinking?'

'Definitely not,' said Alfie. 'Smurble adores me. I've only had him a few days but he's already become my absolute best friend. He's better than the losers in my school, that's for sure.'

Connor and Ethan exchanged a curious glance.

Eventually Alfie halted beside a large, roundish, plump bush.

'Here,' he said. 'Next to this murk-bloom plant. Smurble was running towards me with the stick I'd thrown for him from *that* direction.' He pointed up the path. 'I was standing here. The next thing I knew – **WHUMF!** I was flat out on the ground.'

Ethan, who was standing nearest to the murk-bloom, bent down to peer at the information label planted in the soil beside it. 'Wow!' he said. 'That's cool!'

'What's cool?' asked Connor. 'It just looks like an ordinary bush to me.'

'That *is* an ordinary bush,' said Ethan. 'What's cool is *this* …' He reached down and picked up a small metal object lying on the edge of the stone path. He laid it on his palm. 'See? It's a badge!'

'A badge?' exclaimed Connor excitedly, craning his neck forward to examine the object. 'Is it mine?'

The badge was small and a bright silver colour. On it were the words:

WE ARE STARVILLE STINK BUGS

'*Oh*,' said Connor flatly. 'I had a crazy idea it might be the badge I lost. It's not.'

'What are Starville Stink Bugs?' asked Ethan. 'Some kind of insect?'

'Oh no,' said Alfie quietly. 'It all makes sense now.'

'How come?' asked Ethan.

'That badge,' said Alfie. 'It belongs to one of the Starville Stink Bugs.'

'But who are they?' Ethan asked.

'They're only the meanest gang in my entire school,' laughed Alfie bitterly. 'If they've stolen Smurble I'll never get him back. Oh, this is all my fault!' He kicked savagely at a twig lying on the path, sending it skittering off into the distance.

'What do you mean?' asked Connor.

'It was the last day of term before the summer holidays,' said Alfie. 'Lunchtime. I'd just bought a floozlenut milkshake in the school canteen and I was carrying it to my table, when ...'

'Yes ... ?' said Ethan.

'I tripped.' Alfie winced at the memory. 'Not just a little trip but a proper massive stumble. I hit the floor and my milkshake flew up in the air. And then – **SPLAT!**' He smacked a fist into his open palm. 'The whole thing went all over the Stink Bugs, all three of them. Drenching them.'

'Oh dear,' said Connor. 'Still, it was an accident. I expect they saw the funny side afterwards, didn't they?'

Ethan frowned at his friend. 'For a crime-solving genius you can be ever so slightly dim when it comes to human nature sometimes, mate.'

'No,' said Alfie flatly. 'They didn't see the funny side. They said I was going on their Enemies List.'

'And what happens to people on their Enemies List?' asked Connor.

'Horrible things.'

'I reckon we need to have a little chat with these Stink Bug jokers,' said Ethan. 'Do you know where to find them?'

Alfie nodded. 'In the school holidays, they always hang out in the mall.'

Connor adjusted his glasses, a decisive look on his face. 'Come on, let's get over there.'

Chapter 4
Mall shook up

Towering over the space station's bustling shopping district stood Starville Mall. It was a large, bucket-shaped building,

twenty-five floors of shops, restaurants, 5-D cinemas, and it even had its own track for Venusian racing newts. Around its exterior, huge screens flashed with advertisements for every kind of product, from antigravity carpet slippers to Martian tea. Everything you ever wanted – and even more things you didn't – available to buy 24 hours a day, 365 days a year.

Inside, Connor, Ethan and Alfie threaded their way through the hordes of shoppers and sat on a bench made of white marble.

'I could do with a rest,' said Ethan, wiping his brow with the back of his hand. 'My pockets are weighing me down with all the stuff I bought.'

Connor heaved a small sigh. 'Can I remind you that this wasn't meant to be a shopping trip? We are here on serious detective business.'

'Of course,' said Ethan, rubbing an aching ankle, 'but the prices in the SweetieZone HyperMarket were too good to ignore. Four packets of Salted Wobble Cakes for fifty Starville cents? It's the bargain of the century.'

'Why do you always let your stomach rule your life?' asked Connor wearily.

Ethan shrugged. 'Most of the time it's the only bit of me that knows what it's doing.'

'Can we focus on the case now?' said

Connor impatiently. 'Alfie, you see those three kids over there outside Hudson's House of Humongous Hot Dogs? Are they the Starville Stink Bugs?'

Alfie peered in the direction Connor was pointing and saw three figures lounging in chairs outside one of the many cafes. He nodded. 'That's them. The skinny boy one is called Devlin Smollett,' explained Alfie. 'The girl one is Marsha Brownwater. And the rectangular metal one is Brill-O Padster. He's a robot.'

'Why does a robot need to go to school anyway?' asked Ethan. 'Wouldn't you just program it with all the knowledge it needs straight away?'

Connor shook his head. 'It's good for robots to learn about life from organic beings. It helps them to coexist peacefully with non-robotic people.'

'So what went wrong with this one?'

Connor smiled weakly. 'I guess it started hanging out with the wrong organic beings.'

Ethan nudged Connor. 'So, what's the plan, brainbox?'

'Nothing special,' said Connor. 'I thought we'd go up there and question them. I don't expect any trouble – unless they have something to hide.'

'Aren't you scared of them?' asked Alfie.

Connor gave a shrug. 'Three of them, three of us. And there's loads of people around. I doubt they'd try anything silly. Come on.'

He and Ethan set off towards Hudson's House of Humongous Hot Dogs. Cautiously Alfie followed.

The robot boy Brill-O Padster's shiny metal head swivelled in their direction. 'Alfie Flumpleton approaching,' he droned in his flat electronic voice.

'And he's got backup!' cried Devlin Smollett, jerking a thumb at Connor and Ethan.

'I think we should get out of here right now!' said Marsha Brownwater.

'A logical suggestion,' droned Brill-O.

Without further delay, the three gang members sprang from their seats and dashed off into the throng of shoppers.

'They're on to us! Don't let them get away!' cried Ethan, and raced after them.

Connor and Alfie followed.

The trio of Starville Stink Bugs skidded around a corner and zoomed past the impressive brightly illuminated entrance of Starville Mall Venusian Racing Newt Track. A line of tall, thick-legged racing newts was waiting to be led inside by their trainer. The amphibians watched curiously as the three gang members sped past.

Ethan thundered around the corner at top speed, almost colliding with a stall selling musical popcorn. He dodged and weaved between clumps of shoppers, his heart pounding and his lungs almost bursting. Before very long, he had to stop and catch his breath.

'It's no good,' he muttered to himself as he slid to his knees, his pulse throbbing in his ears. 'I was made for short bursts of speed, not marathons.'

A sudden **CROAKING** sound made him look up.

A huge newt was standing beside him. Sitting on its back and clutching a set of reins were Connor and Alfie.

'Quickly!' hissed Connor. 'Climb on board. Before his owner realises he's missing!'

With long, loping strides, the Venusian racing newt galloped along the busy mall, drawing confused looks from shoppers. On

its back, the three boys clung to the reins with whitening knuckles.

'They're trying to reach that exit,' said Connor, pointing at a far-off doorway towards which the three Starville Stink Bugs were racing. 'We need to head them off.' He yanked on the newt's reins and the enormous scaly creature gave a fresh burst of speed.

'Where did you learn to ride a Venusian newt?' asked Ethan.

'I didn't,' said Connor. 'My uncle Brian has an ostrich farm and I used to ride those sometimes when we went to visit. I assumed the principle was the same.'

By now, the racing newt was gaining on the three gang members. Suddenly the three Stink Bugs changed course, swerving to avoid a Starville Mega Lottery kiosk and knocking over an elderly couple laden with shopping bags. The old couple picked themselves up and shook angry fists after the retreating trio.

'They went in that cheese shop!' cried Alfie, bouncing along on the newt's back. 'Did you see?'

'Just as I hoped,' said Ethan with satisfaction.

'Why did you want them to go in there?'

'Because with luck they'll be going too fast to stop themselves in time.'

'In time for what?' asked Alfie.

There was a sudden deafening **SQUEL-CHING** sound.

'In time for *that*,' said Ethan.

Dismounting from the newt, they rushed into the Cheese Superstore to find a huge vat of molten cheese the size of a swimming pool. A sign above it read:

MERCURY FONDUE

THE HOTTEST MELTED CHEESE IN THE SOLAR SYSTEM

The three gang members were stuck fast in the hot sludgy liquid, unable to haul themselves out.

'Help me,' droned Brill-O, blobs of molten cheese spurting from his joints. 'My circuits are seizing up.'

'And I'm allergic to dairy foods!' groaned Marsha, her face turning green.

'And I hate bloomin' cheese!' moaned Devlin. 'Even pizza!'

'First, tell us what you did with this kid's Synthpet,' demanded Ethan.

'What Synthpet?' droned Brill-O. 'I know nothing about any missing Synthpet, you squelchy lump of organic slime.'

'Well, one of you dropped this badge at the botanical gardens in the exact place where Alfie's pet was stolen,' said Ethan, tossing the Stink Bugs badge for Brill-O to catch.

'We haven't been there for weeks,' said Brill-O, seizing the badge before it fell into the cheesy gloop. 'Last time we went, a huge plant from Cygnus B made a grab for me. I got soil up my extraction filter. I did not enjoy the experience.'

'Why are you always out to get us, Flumpleton?' demanded Devlin, scraping a lump of cheese from his ear.

'Yeah,' agreed Marsha. 'We never did

anything to you.'

Slowly the three gang members hauled themselves from the vat of oozing cheese. 'Come on, guys,' said Devlin, with all the dignity he could muster. 'Let's go to my granny's house. She said she'd bake us Martian squitch-fruit scones if we mowed her lawn and tidied her shed.'

As one, the Stink Bugs turned and strode from the shop, the gloopy cheese squelching in their shoes.

Ethan turned to Alfie. 'I thought you said this gang hated you after you accidentally spilt that floozlenut shake on them?'

Alfie shrugged. 'Yeah, well, perhaps I did that on purpose because they wouldn't let me join their stupid gang.' He stalked out of the shop moodily.

'OK,' said Connor. 'One thing we know for certain. The Starville Stink Bugs did *not* steal Smurble.'

'How can you be so sure?' asked Ethan.

'Because the robot said he knew nothing about any attempt to steal Smurble, plus they haven't been to the botanical gardens in weeks. Robots don't lie! It's part of their programming. They're incapable of it.'

Ethan suddenly frowned. 'Hey! He called me a squelchy lump of organic slime!'

'I guess that's how robots see us,' said Connor.

'All of which means we've made exactly zero progress on the case so far,' sighed Ethan.

'Not quite,' said Connor. 'We've learned that we can't always trust what our client says.'

Suddenly they heard Alfie calling from outside the shop.

'Guys! Come quickly! You've got to see this!'

The **Space Detectives** found Alfie standing beside a fast-food stall called **TASTES OF CYGNUS B**. He was trembling all over with rage.

'Look!' said Alfie, jabbing a finger at a menu board standing in front of the stall.

On the menu board were the words:

TODAY'S SPECIAL – FOR ONE DAY ONLY!

And beside that an illustration of a strange creature with four legs, a bill like a duck, long ears, a pair of antennae and a long, scaly tail.

It looked exactly like Smurble.

Chapter 5
Trash talk

The creature serving behind the counter at the **TASTES OF CYGNUS B** stall was a sort of large transparent blob known as a Saturnian globuloid.

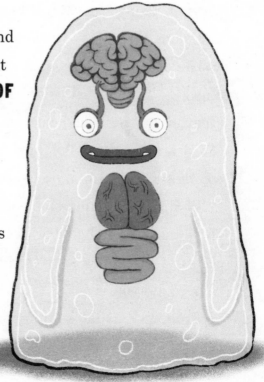

It smiled as the three boys approached.

'What can I get you, lads?'

'You can get me my Synthpet!' hooted Alfie. 'You better not have cooked him!'

The globuloid narrowed its two small eyes. 'Sorry, son. I don't follow you.'

Ethan rotated the blackboard towards the bemused stallholder. 'This dish you're serving. Today's special? It looks exactly like a missing pet we're trying to find.'

The globuloid gave a low, warbling chuckle. 'There must be some mistake! That creature on the blackboard isn't a Synthpet. It's a short-haired flotchgobber. They're a common farm animal on Cygnus B.'

'Well, by an amazing coincidence, this short-haired flotchgobber looks just like the creature we're looking for,' said Ethan. 'Where did you get it?'

'From my usual supplier on Cygnus B,

of course.'

Connor frowned and adjusted his glasses. 'Could you please give us their details so we can ask them some questions?'

'Of course,' replied the globuloid, 'but Cygnus B is 730 million light years away, so unless you have access to a faster-than-light starship, it might take you *rather* a long time to make the trip.'

Connor rubbed his chin thoughtfully. 'What do you do with the inedible bits of the animals you cook?'

'All the bones and leftover bits get automatically removed by the electronic grill,' said the globuloid. 'They go in the central market waste container at the back of the stall.'

Connor looked at Ethan and Alfie. 'We should check it for Smurble's microchip. It's the only way to know for sure.'

The waste container was large and made of metal. It looked like an enormous skip. Alfie and the two **Space Detectives** scaled the service ladder on the outside of the container and stood on its thin metal

rim staring down into the vast jumble of waste within – empty packaging, bones, fur, soggy cardboard and a hundred different types of decaying food, all of it floating on a deep layer of foul-smelling water. The stink, hot and sickly, stung their eyes.

'What does your tracker say?' Ethan asked Alfie.

Alfie consulted his watch. 'Hard to tell. The signal's still really fuzzy. We should probably get closer.'

Connor sighed. 'Come on then. Let's get this over with.' He stepped down on to the ladder on the inside of the container and climbed down towards the filthy refuse.

'Wish I hadn't put my best trainers on this morning,' muttered Alfie.

Nearby they found an old wooden door floating on the waste that seemed stable

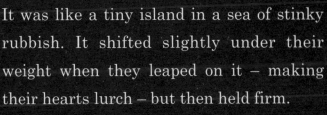

It was like a tiny island in a sea of stinky rubbish. It shifted slightly under their weight when they leaped on it – making their hearts lurch – but then held firm.

Alfie swept his arm back and forth, scanning the waste for signs of Smurble's microchip with his watch. With his other hand, he held his nose. Ethan and Connor held their own noses too.

'Nubbink bo var.'

'Whad?' asked Ethan.

'By bed nubbink bo var. Bo bign ov Burble's dip,' said Alfie.

'I dan't umberdand whad you're daying.'

'Whad?'

'Dop olding dor dose.'

'Whad?'

Ethan sighed and stopped holding his nose. Immediately the horrid stink assaulted his nostrils. He grimaced. 'I said stop holding your nose. Any sign of Smurble's chip?'

Alfie stopped holding his nose and checked his watch. 'Nope. I don't think it's in here, is it?' He grimaced at the awful smell. 'Come on. No point hanging around in this place.'

They were about to make for the ladder again when there was a deafening buzzing sound and a huge wave tore towards them across the filthy water. They watched, astounded, as an enormous fly the size of a horse burst from the trash, sending fragments flying in all directions, and zoomed off happily into the sky, oblivious to their presence.

Before they could leap to safety, the wave smashed into the door they were standing on, upending it and sending the three boys plummeting head first into the smelly water.

'**Bleeeeuugh!**' said Ethan.
'**Eeeeeuuuch!**' said Connor.
'**Uuurrrrggh!**' said Alfie.

They thrashed their limbs in the foul water, which was surprisingly deep, each boy clinging desperately on to some nearby floating bit of refuse.

His face a mask of disgust, Connor gestured with his free hand to the nearest service ladder. 'Come on. Let's paddle towards that.'

Suddenly the stinking trash-filled ooze began to churn and froth. Thirty pairs of tiny eyes broke the surface of the water,

each accompanied by a small triangular fin. The eyes fixed on Connor, Ethan and Alfie – and then began to streak towards them through the water.

'Trash piranhas!' yelled Connor. 'Let's get moving!'

He started to paddle furiously towards the ladder.

Ethan and Alfie paddled after Connor as quickly as they could. Ethan risked a quick glance back over his shoulder and saw thirty tiny mouths filled with pointed teeth snapping hungrily.

Connor made it to the ladder first. He scrambled halfway up and held out his hand. Alfie lunged for it and Connor pulled him to safety.

The shoal of hungry trash piranhas was gaining on Ethan. He could hear the **SNAP** of each fish's tiny but terrible jaws. Legs thrashing frantically, he hurled himself towards the ladder as a dozen trash piranhas shot from the water like flying fish, teeth gleaming like tiny daggers.

Just in time, Connor seized Ethan's hand and yanked him up the ladder, the snapping jaws of the leaping trash piranhas mere centimetres from his foot. Eyes blazing madly, the fish plopped back into the smelly water as all three boys scrambled up the ladder to safety. Once on the container's metal rim, they slid quickly down the outside service ladder and collapsed in a soggy, stinky, grateful heap on the ground.

Ethan took off one of his shoes and poured out a stream of evil-smelling water. 'Is it OK with you guys if we never do that ever, ever, ever again?'

'Suits me,' groaned Alfie.

Connor took off his glasses and wiped the

filthy water from the lenses with his thumb.
'So, here's where our investigation currently
stands. We don't think the Starville Stink
Bugs took Smurble. Alfie's tracker can't tell
us anything definite and the fast-food stall
was just using flotchgobbers from Cygnus
B. We've reached a dead end, haven't we?'

'Oh, *brilliant!*' sighed Ethan. He nudged
Alfie. 'Isn't there anything else you can
remember? Just the tiniest detail that might

help us crack the case?'

Alfie snorted. 'What am I supposed to do? You're meant to be the detectives, aren't you? You figure it out.'

Ethan peeled a soggy crisp packet from his hair. 'So we start the investigation again. Fine. At least today can't get any worse now.'

'That's just where you're wrong, my lad!' barked a gruff voice.

They looked up and found themselves facing a squad of brawny, dark-uniformed Mall Security Guards.

'Right,' yelled the Head Guard, a woman with the muscles of a bodybuilder and the friendly manner of a venomous snake with backache. She quickly clapped three pairs of heavy electro-handcuffs around their wrists. 'You're under arrest, all three of you, for hijacking a racing newt!'

Chapter 6
Cellmates

Ignoring their protests, the Mall Security
Guards bundled Connor, Ethan and Alfie
into a holding cell at the Mall Security
Station.

'Oh, you're in trouble!' laughed the Head
Guard. She swung the cell door shut with a
clang and eyed them through its tiny
rectangular window. 'I haven't arrested any
thieves for ages so I'm really gonna enjoy
this! I expect you'll end up serving six
hundred years in a high-security detention
cube! You little rotters!'

'You don't understand!' groaned Connor, rubbing the sore skin where the heavy handcuffs had dug into his wrist. 'We were investigating a crime ourselves! A pet has been stolen …'

'Well, you'd know all about theft, you newt-rustlers!' snapped the Head Guard.

'We didn't steal the newt,' pleaded Alfie. 'We just borrowed it. It was an emergency!'

'Quiet!' barked the Head Guard. 'I've had enough of your whining! What is it with kids today, eh? It was different back in my day. If you misbehaved when I was a nipper, a police-bot would just disintegrate you. What we need these days is a few more disintegrations. Especially for evil hooligans like you! Well, don't you worry! I'll make sure you feel the full force of the law when it comes time for you to be sentenced, and *then*—'

71

She paused as one of her colleagues whispered something in her ear.

Connor, Ethan and Alfie exchanged puzzled glances.

'Ah,' said the Head Guard to her colleague. 'I see. Thank you very much.'

The cell door suddenly swung open.

'You're free to go, lads,' said the Head Guard with a sickly smile. 'My assistant here tells me that one of you is the son of Fred Frumpleton, Head of Security for the whole of Starville. I don't want to get in his bad books. So please accept my apologies and do take a free toffee from the front desk on the way out with our compliments. Have a nice day!'

Ethan gave a whoop of joy. 'Fantastic! Is your dad really Head of Security for the whole of Starville, Alfie?'

Alfie nodded coolly. 'Yeah. Comes in

handy sometimes.'

As he, Connor and Ethan were leaving the cell, Alfie turned to the Head Guard and said, 'Actually, not that one.' He pointed at Connor.

'You're the boss!' the Head Guard replied, shoving Connor back inside, slamming the door and disappearing into her office.

'Hey!' shouted Connor in confusion from inside the cell.

'What?' demanded Ethan. 'Why isn't Connor being released?'

Alfie folded his arms and cocked his head to one side. 'I'm not massively impressed with the amateurish way you and your friend are investigating this case. I reckon this will help focus your mind a bit.'

'What are you on about?'

'It couldn't be simpler,' said Alfie. 'Until you find Smurble, Connor stays in that cell.'

'But that makes no flipping sense whatsoever!' exploded Ethan. 'Connor's the brains of this outfit! How am I supposed to do this investigation without him? You'd be better off locking me up and letting Connor try to find Smurble by himself.'

'Not my problem,' said Alfie. 'So you better get on with finding my Synthpet. Guard, remind me what time the rocket bus leaves for the Detention Swamps of Pluto again?'

'Midnight!' shouted out the gruff voice of the Head Guard.

Ethan banged a hand on the cell door and squinted through the narrow opening. Connor was staring back in bewilderment.

'You hear all that?'

'Yes,' said Connor. 'It's pretty outrageous!'

'Don't worry, pal. I'll have you out of there in no time.'

Connor gave him a cheery thumbs up. 'Of course you will. I don't doubt you for a second.' Ethan couldn't help noticing that the fingers of Connor's other hand were crossed.

Alfie smirked. 'If you want to see your friend again you'd better stop wasting time and get detecting, hadn't you?'

Ethan turned away from the cell door. 'At least I've got a friend,' he muttered, pushing past Alfie and heading back out into the swarming streets of Starville.

Where should he even start? Looking for a single lost creature on a space station filled with thousands of alien life forms seemed an impossible task. He needed to think!

Chapter 7
Coughs and robbers

Head in hands, Ethan sat on the bench in the small park opposite the *Space Detectives* building, a place he and Connor often visited when they needed to clear their heads and approach a case from a fresh angle. Today though, Ethan felt all out of fresh angles.

Not only had they failed to make progress on the case of the missing Synthpet, he mused darkly, but now Connor had been locked up, and there was a very real chance that Ethan would never see his friend again.

Eyes screwed shut and one hand tapping his forehead to wake up his brain cells, Ethan tried to rearrange the facts of the case in his mind, like a person shuffling the pieces of a difficult jigsaw to see if they would finally fit together in a way that made sense.

Nothing. Ethan couldn't help thinking he was missing a really important piece of this puzzle.

Maybe he was trying too hard? Solutions didn't always come into your head when you wanted them to. Sometimes they popped out of nowhere, surprising you. Ethan leaned back on the bench and tried to let his mind go blank. But once it was blank, it stayed blank, and no amazing ideas came. *OK, fine*, he thought. Maybe what his brain needed was a hit of sugar? He reached into his pocket and drew out a small Salted Wobble Cake. He unwrapped it and took a thoughtful bite.

Mmm. Yum.

Ethan felt a gentle tapping against his right ankle. He looked down and saw a small green plant prodding him with a long, spiky leaf. This was a snaffle-shrub. They were a common sight on Starville, sprouting through cracks in the pavement the way dandelions and daisies did on Earth. But unlike those Earth weeds, snaffle-shrubs had jaws, rather like Venus flytraps, and when they sensed food was nearby, they could reach out for it with their spindly leaves.

'All right,' laughed Ethan. 'Calm down, mate.' He tore off a small bit of his Salted Wobble Cake and dropped it into the snaffle-shrub's tiny green jaws. The plant chewed the morsel of food gratefully for a few seconds before swallowing it with a tiny gulp. Suddenly the snaffle-shrub began to tremble. Its leaves waved in an agitated manner and it made a series of noises that sounded like some botanical version of coughing.

'Eat it too fast, did you?' said Ethan. 'Yeah, I do that all the time. Connor's always having a go at me about it.'

The snaffle-shrub gave a final cough and expelled a mouthful of semi-digested Salted Wobble Cake on to the pavement at Ethan's feet.

'Yuck!' cried Ethan. 'I've never seen a plant throw up before! That's disgusting!'

He shuffled along the bench away from the plant, but as he did so the glint of something shiny caught his eye. In the middle of the small pile of chewed-up Salted Wobble Cake that the snaffle-shrub had just spat out sat a gleaming metal disc. Gingerly, and with a grimace on his face, Ethan plucked it out between his thumb and forefinger and held it up to the light. It was a badge and on it were the words:

World's Greatest Detective

Connor's missing badge!

Of course! Connor must have dropped it here the last time they were sitting on this bench together and the snaffle-shrub must have swallowed it! It all made sense!

He stood up, thinking how pleased Connor would be when he told him about the badge – and suddenly sat back down on the bench with a heavy bump.

Wait a minute!

In his head, the pieces of the jigsaw had finally fallen into place.

Maybe they'd been going about the case all wrong. This investigation was certainly different from any cases the **Space Detectives** had solved before, and Ethan realised he needed to go right back to the beginning. There was something he'd missed the first time ...

Typing with furious speed, he began to compose a text message to Alfie.

MEET ME AT THE
BOTANICAL GARDENS
RIGHT NOW!

Chapter 8
Plant potty

The letterbox-sized window in Connor's cell door slid open, revealing the leering eyes of the Head Guard.

'No sign of that tubby little friend of yours,' she sniggered. 'And only a few short hours until midnight! Dear oh dear! My, what a fun time you'll have in the Detention Swamps of Pluto!'

'Fun?' said Connor with a small note of hope. 'Are they fun then? These Detention Swamps? Because the name doesn't sound very fun.'

'Of course they're not fun!' cackled the Head Guard. 'I was being sarcastic! They wake you at half past five every morning and make you take a six-mile trek through the Stinking Slush Mires, and then you spend the rest of the day sewing waistcoats for Martian sewer-worms out of dried Plutonian Prickle-Leaves! And all you have to eat is Plutonian porridge, which is so dry and tasteless it's like eating a minced birthday card.'

'Oh,' said Connor. 'I see. Are you always this sarcastic?'

'Pretty much,' said the Head Guard.

'And what do your friends think of you being this sarcastic the whole time?'

'Friends?' said the Head Guard. 'I don't really have any.'

'No friends?' said Connor. 'Really? No one at all?'

'Why do I need friends when I have my collection?'

'What collection?'

The Head Guard glanced swiftly up and down the corridor to make sure no one was about. 'If I let you out to show you my collection do you promise not to try to run away?'

'Yes, all right,' said Connor. 'I promise I won't run away.'

The Head Guard unlocked the cell door, not noticing that once again Connor had his fingers crossed.

She led him to a cramped office where every spare centimetre was jammed with plants of a hundred different varieties. There were plants in pots, on shelves, climbing the walls and even some kind of strange vines dangling from the ceiling and swaying. It was more jungle than office, thought Connor. He half-expected to see parrots flying overhead, or maybe even a Snarltoothed Grizloid padding through the undergrowth.

'So,' said the Head Guard eagerly, 'what do you think?'

Connor wanted to say it was the most bonkers room he had ever seen but sensed this would not go down well. 'I think it's … very unique,' he said politely.

'Isn't it?' agreed the Head Guard. 'I reckon plants are far more interesting than boring old *people*. Look at this one! It's new!'

She showed him a large green plant whose leaves were folded together like jaws. As she waved her hand at it, the leaves leaned towards her, almost like a cat wanting to be stroked.

'This one's a murk-bloom from Cygnus B. They get lonely, you know, so you have to show them lots of affection.'

She made a gruesome kissy face at the plant.

Connor saw his chance. Swiftly he pulled one of the hanging green vines away from the ceiling, looped it around the Head Guard's arms and tied it securely with a tight knot. Then he dashed at top speed towards the open window and made a dive for it.

In an instant, as Connor was sailing through mid-air towards the window, the murk-bloom suddenly opened a pair of enormous jaw-like leaves and caught hold of his foot like a frog catching a fly. He crashed to the floor in a painful heap.

The Head Guard flexed her muscles and the green vine binding them snapped easily and fell to the floor. She unclasped the plant's jaws from around Connor's ankle and gave a throaty chuckle. 'I think it likes you!'

Chapter 9
In pod
we trust

The gates to Starville Botanical Gardens were locked when Ethan and Alfie arrived.

'Why are we here?' asked Alfie grumpily. 'Like I told you in your office, I searched the whole place.'

'Not quite everywhere,' said Ethan. 'I reckon there's one last place we should look.'

'So how do we get inside? You have some whizzy detective gizmo that can let you walk through solid walls?'

'No need,' said Ethan. 'We'll just have a word with the anteater.' He banged his hand against the ticket booth. Its shutter retracted and the anteater appeared. It was wearing space-themed pyjamas.

'What's going on?' it bellowed. 'It's my bedtime!'

'We need to go in,' said Ethan. 'And quick! It's an emergency!'

'Don't care,' said the anteater. 'We're shut. Clear off.'

'Stop messing about,' said Alfie. 'This is vital!'

'And it's vital that I follow the rule that stops you getting inside!' countered the anteater. 'So there.'

'What about the rule that says botanical gardens employees aren't allowed to keep pets in their ticket booths?' said Ethan. 'You have a turtle in there, don't you?'

The anteater gulped. 'Not little Jackie! He's my best mate in all the world. You wouldn't let them take my little Jackie away from me! I'd be lost without him.'

'Well, I'm trying to save *my* best mate in all the world,' said Ethan. 'Isn't that worth bending your rules for?'

'You need to save a friend?'

'Yes!'

There was a short pause and then a click, and the gate to the botanical gardens swung open.

'Everyone needs friends, don't they?'

said the anteater. 'Good luck!'

Once through the gates, Ethan and Alfie hurried along one of the many snaking paths that criss-crossed the floor of the gardens. The air was warm and scented and filled with the gentle music of night insects.

Alfie grinned at Ethan. 'Smart move. But how did you know that botanical gardens employees aren't allowed to keep pets at work? Have you memorised the rules and regulations of every public building in Starville?'

'No,' said Ethan, 'but it was a pretty safe bet. There aren't many businesses that let people bring their pets to work. Which is a pity. Probably be a lot less stress in the universe if people could.'

Soon, they arrived once more at the scene of the crime. Alfie looked up and down the path. Everything seemed eerily quiet and still. He raised his eyebrows at Ethan. 'We're here. So? What did we miss? I don't see anything different.'

'You will,' said Ethan. He stepped over the low barrier separating the vegetation from the path and beckoned Alfie to follow. He parted a thick curtain of green fronds hanging from above and pointed at a huge green pod nestling among the other plants.

Alfie gaped. 'What's that?'

'Those are the jaws of a fully grown murk-bloom plant from Cygnus B,' said Ethan. 'And if I'm right, your Synthpet is inside.'

'What?' Alfie tapped the side of the bright green pod. 'In here? It's hard as iron! We should have brought an electric saw or laser cutters.'

'No need,' said Ethan. 'All we need is a Salted Wobble Cake and a little kindness.'

'I don't understand,' said Alfie.

'No,' agreed Ethan. 'But you will.'

Bending down, Ethan read from the label next to the plant that he'd noticed earlier that day but hadn't realised was important because he'd been distracted by the Stink Bug badge. '*The murk-bloom from Cygnus B is almost unique in the plant kingdom because in order to thrive it requires not just water, soil and sunlight, but also* friendship.

On its home world it frequently befriends creatures of many different species such as warbler monkeys, blue-tailed tree-prawns and flotchgobbers, making a comfortable nest for its friend to snooze in inside its great green pod ...'

Alfie's eyebrows leaped halfway up his forehead. 'What?'

'Do you get it now?' said Ethan. 'When this murk-bloom spotted Smurble, it mistook him for a flotchgobber from its home planet *and it wanted to be friends with him*! The jaws of its pod must have accidentally hit you on the head when it opened up to let Smurble inside!'

Alfie banged his hand on the side of the pod. 'You mean Smurble's inside this thing? I hope he's OK in there.'

'Whoa! Calm down!' said Ethan, stroking the pod. 'I'm sure Smurble's fine.'

'So how do we get him out?'

'Like so.'

Ethan took a Salted Wobble Cake from his pocket and removed it from its wrapper. 'If I'm right, murk-blooms hate salt just as much as their smaller cousins, the snaffle-shrubs.'

He rubbed the cake against the pod, smearing the sticky icing across its surface. Almost immediately, the pod began to tremble.

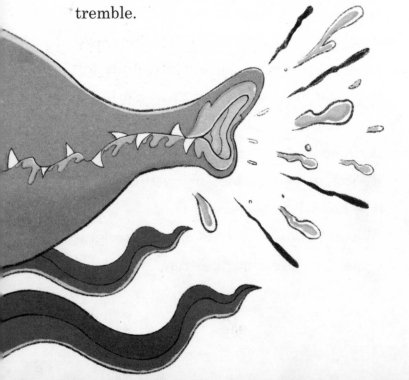

'Probably best to take cover,' advised Ethan. 'It looks like it's about to ...'

BLEEEEUUUURRRRGGGHHHH!

With a mighty retch, the two jaws of the pod opened and expelled a large furry lump, which sailed through the air and landed gently on a soft patch of orange Martian grass. The furry lump unfolded itself, revealing legs, a duck's bill, two long ears, a swishing reptilian tail and two twitching antennae.

'Smurble!' cried Alfie, and ran over to embrace his Synthpet. Smurble clicked and squeaked with delight and licked Alfie's face with his long sticky tongue.

Ethan looked at his watch nervously. 'While it's great that you two friends are back together, there's a friend of mine who could do with help pretty urgently! Let's get moving!'

Chapter 10
Friends reunited

It was nearly midnight and the last few passengers had boarded the rocket bus to Pluto outside Starville Mall. The driver glanced at her watch, closed the door and fired up the bus's engine.

'Wait!' cried a voice. 'Don't go yet!'

The driver looked in her mirror and saw a hover-scooter zoom to a halt beside the bus. On it were two boys and a very strange-looking animal. The shorter of the two boys leaped off the vehicle and slapped a hand a few times on the bus's door.

'Check your communicator!' he yelled, pointing to the driver's personal communicator device, which lay on the dashboard. She did so and found the following message:

TO: ROCKET BUS DRIVER A. BURTON
RELEASE PRISONER CONNOR
CRAKE *IMMEDIATELY!*
SIGNED: FRED FLUMPLETON, HEAD
OF SECURITY, STARVILLE

The driver got up and walked to a seat near the back of the bus where Connor sat, his wrists bound by electronic handcuffs. She entered the combination into the handcuffs' keypad and they sprang open.

'Looks like you ain't going to Pluto today after all,' she said.

'Mate!' cried Ethan, seeing his friend step down off the bus. 'Glad you could make it!' Connor wasn't a hugger so instead the two boys exchanged the special *Space Detective* handshake they had invented, which was a complicated affair involving twirling fingers and owl hoots.

Once that was completed, Ethan briefly outlined the solution to the case.

Connor looked over at Alfie and Smurble and adjusted his glasses thoughtfully. 'Yes, of course. The Head Guard has a smaller version of the murk-bloom. It attempted to make friends with my foot. Obviously it's an extremely emotional type of plant.'

'No hard feelings, eh, Connor?' said Alfie as he scratched Smurble's ears. 'This little guy means everything to me. You understand why I had to keep you locked up?'

Before Connor could reply, Ethan hooted in outrage. 'No hard feelings? After what you've done we ought to send you on a one-way trip to Pluto, pal!'

Connor raised a hand. 'It's OK, Ethan. I get it. Alfie was frightened about what might have happened to his pet, and fear makes people do silly things.'

'Does this mean you're going to be a bit less of a jerk to people now, Alfie?' said Ethan, raising his eyebrows.

'Definitely,' said Alfie. 'I feel really bad

about how I behaved towards you and the Starville Stink Bugs.'

'Maybe there's something you could do to make up for it,' said Connor with a faint smile.

Alfie nodded. 'Do you know, I think there might be!'

The following evening was a busy night at Starville Mall Venusian Racing Newt Track. A vast crowd of people were crammed into the enormous stadium to watch the 7 p.m. race. Music blared, racegoers chatted excitedly and the air was filled with enticing scents of fast food from a thousand different worlds.

At 7 p.m. precisely, the ten racing newts and their riders gathered at the starting line, the eager newts pawing at the ground with their huge front claws. A loud buzzer sounded and the race began. With a frantic burst of motion, all ten newts lunged forward and began to scamper madly around the track.

Watching from a luxurious private balcony in the stand were Connor, Ethan, Alfie, Smurble and the three Starville Stink Bugs: Devlin, Marsha and Brill-O. Each was clutching a betting slip containing details of the newt each of them had backed to win the race.

'Come on, Green Lightning!' yelled Marsha.

'Come on, Scaly Sam!' called Ethan.

'It is my wish for the competitor known as The Great Crested Whirlwind to triumph,' droned Brill-O at his highest volume setting.

The newts sprinted around the track at impressive speed, the colourful costumes of their jockeys streaking past like fireworks.

Connor looked at the others and broke

out into a broad grin. The visit to the racing-newt track seemed to be proving a success. It had taken a little work to persuade Devlin, Marsha and Brill-O to come here and hang out with Alfie. But now, much to his relief, everyone was getting on well and having a lot of fun.

'Come on, Pond King!' shouted Alfie.

'Come on, Emerald Toes!' yelled Connor.

'Come on, Newtron-Bomb!' called Devlin.

A bell rang indicating the race was entering the final lap. The crowd buzzed with anticipation as everyone sat forward in their seats and waited to see who would win.

The pack of newts looked neck and neck for some time until one amphibian whose rider wore bright yellow shorts broke from the pack and made a frantic dash for the winning line.

'Come on!' called Alfie. 'Come on!'

The newt with the yellow-shorted rider stretched its long neck as far as it would go and passed first over the winning line.

'And the winner,' echoed a voice from a loudspeaker, 'is Number Fifteen – Pond King!'

The crowd erupted in cheers. Victory music blared.

'I've won!' cried Alfie. 'I bet on Pond King! I've just won a hundred Starville dollars!'

'Well done, pal!' said Devlin, clapping him on the back.

'You have proven skilful at choosing the fastest racing newt,' droned Brill-O. 'My congratulations!'

'I'm going to order one of those massive platters of zap-burgers and slurp-dogs for us all to share with my winnings,' said Alfie. 'Let's celebrate!' He quickly typed an order into the electronic pad set into the arm of his seat.

The food arrived swiftly and the six children began to tuck in with great enthusiasm, even Brill-O, whose stomach mechanism had been adapted to allow him to enjoy human food.

While the others gorged themselves on this feast, Ethan beckoned Connor aside.

'Yep?' asked Connor.

Ethan rummaged in his pocket and handed

Connor something. 'I believe this is yours.'

'My World's Greatest Detective badge!' cried Connor in delight. 'Amazing! Where was it?'

'Inside a plant, of course,' said Ethan. 'It's where most things seem to end up these days.'

Connor handed it back to Ethan.

'What's this for?'

'I think you should keep it,' said Connor.

'Why?'

'You've earned it.'

'Aw, thanks, mate!' said Ethan and, grinning broadly, he fixed the badge to the front of his shirt. He gazed out over the racetrack and through the great glass dome that surrounded Starville, into the endless blackness of space. There really was nothing better than solving mysteries with his best friend. Being a *Space Detective* was cosmically cool.

COULD YOU BE A SPACE DETECTIVE?

WERE YOU PAYING ATTENTION?

TAKE THE QUIZ AND FIND OUT!

1. Which animal parts is Smurble made of?
      a) cat, rabbit, duck, crocodile
      b) cat, hippopotamus, goose, crocodile
      c) cat, rabbit, ostrich, alligator

2. Which item did Connor lose?
      a) glasses
      b) watch
      c) badge

3. Which delicious treats did Ethan get as an absolute bargain in the mall?
      a) Salted Wobble Cakes
      b) Ginger and Spoffleblob Muffins
      c) Whippleplofter Fancies

4. Who did Alfie think had stolen Smurble?
      a) Pongo Birds
      b) Smelly Wombats
      c) Stink Bugs

5. Which creatures attacked the Space Detectives in the waste container?

a) trash dolphins
b) trash piranhas
c) trash squid

6. Who got left in the prison cell?

a) Alfie
b) Connor
c) Ethan

7. Which pet does the anteater working at the botanical gardens have?

a) turtle
b) hamster
c) dog

8. Which plant had taken Smurble?

a) Cygnus B murk-bloom
b) snaffle-shrub
c) Neptunian shark-daisy

9. Which Venusian racing newt won at the end?

a) Scaly Sam
b) Green Lightning
c) Pond King

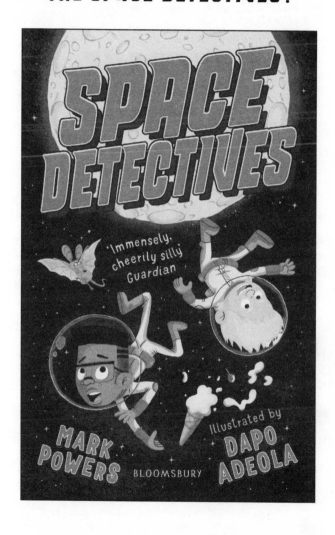

PROLOGUE

The lone figure stared at the laptop screen and gave a chuckle.

In the darkened room, it was impossible to tell whether the figure was young or old, male or female, human or alien. But there was no mistaking the pure evil in its laugh.

The task that lay ahead was difficult. A few details remained to be checked. But if the plan succeeded, the result would be unimaginable terror ...

A muffled voice called, interrupting the figure's thoughts. The figure closed the laptop and went downstairs for dinner. It was fish fingers.

Chapter 1
Welcome to Starville

It was another perfect day on Starville – the most astonishing place in the galaxy. A gigantic space station, Starville sailed silently overhead in orbit around the Earth and was home to over a million humans and aliens. It was a single, vast city brimming with skyscrapers, lush green parks and even a sparkling artificial sea, all enclosed by a huge and incredibly strong glass dome. Seen through a telescope from the world below, it looked like a gleaming snow globe gliding majestically through the night sky.

At the edge of a wide, tree-lined square near the centre of Starville's fanciest shopping district, two ten-year-old human boys stood behind an ice cream stall. One was tall, gawky and looked a bit like an ostrich wearing glasses. His name was Connor. The other was short, squat and constantly bristling with energy like a terrier. This was Ethan.

The square was full of humans and aliens enjoying the sunshine. Business at the ice cream stall was brisk.

'Wow,' said Ethan as he watched their latest customers, a family of tall, two-legged, blue-skinned, cow-like creatures, walk away licking their lips. 'Those Neptunian Cow People really love our Extra Minty Grapefruit and Smoky Bacon flavour! That's the fifth lot we've sold to them today.'

Connor adjusted his glasses, a sure sign there was something on his mind. 'Actually, Ethan, the Cow People are from *Pluto*, not Neptune. You should try to remember that. We wouldn't want to offend any of our customers.'

Ethan had to laugh. 'Give me a chance, mate! We've only been on Starville a week. I haven't learned all the alien races who live here yet.'

'Well, you could have memorised them all
on the rocket trip up here, like I did,' said
Connor. 'What were you doing?'

Ethan shrugged. 'Looking out of the

window and going, **"Blimey, I'm on a flipping rocket!"**

That and eating the cakes my mum baked for the trip. You can't learn everything in books, you know. Sometimes you need to just look around you. Or taste around you.' He scooped a stray blob of ice cream from the machine's dispenser nozzle with the end of his finger and popped it in his mouth.

Connor glared at him. 'For the last time, stop doing that. It's unhygienic. You'll get us closed down.'

'Oh yeah,' said Ethan. 'Sorry.'

'Anyway, I'd recommend getting to know all the different alien races now we're here,' said Connor. 'It might be handy for a case.'

'A case!' said Ethan, staring off into the distance. 'That's what we need!'

'Tell me about it,' grumbled Connor, folding his arms. 'I hardly think standing around all day selling ice cream is a good use of our skills.'

These boys were more than just ice cream sellers. They were **detectives**! Back home on Earth, Connor and Ethan had solved many mysteries together in their spare time, such as finding their head teacher's missing antique letter opener (long story short: magpie). As a result, the two boys had got rather good at finding the solutions to people's thorny problems. So when Ethan's Uncle Nick had invited them to spend the long summer holidays working on his ice cream stall on Starville, the pair had accepted instantly. This was their chance to be *Space Detectives*!

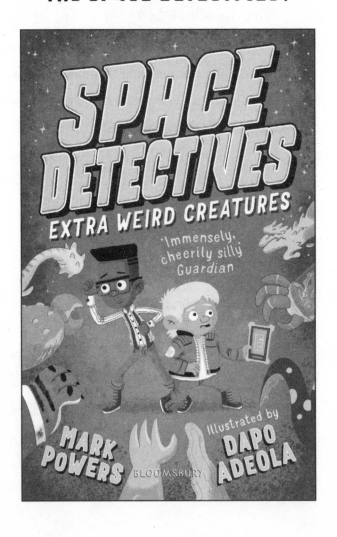

Mark Powers has been making up ridiculous stories since primary school. He grew up in North Wales and now lives in Manchester. If he could go anywhere in space he'd like to go to the Planet of the Doughnuts (that is a thing, isn't it?).

Dapo Adeola is a total sci-fi enthusiast who loves creating characters for books and animation. He grew up in South London and now resides in East London, which according to him is about as close to another world as you're gonna get here on Earth.

LOOK OUT FOR

Dan is a teddy bear.
He's made for hugging.
Aw, so cute, right?
WRONG!

Dan's so strong he can CRUSH CARS.
But what makes him a FAULTY TOY
could make him the PERFECT SPY.

With a robot police rabbit
and one seriously angry doll, Dan is in
a **TOP SECRET TEAM** designed to
STOP CRIMINALS in their tracks.

It's all up to the
SPY TOYS!